Elias Sill Hawley

Historical Sketch of Major Joseph Hawley of Northampton, Mass.

1723-1788 - Vol. 1

Elias Sill Hawley

Historical Sketch of Major Joseph Hawley of Northampton, Mass.
1723-1788 - Vol. 1

ISBN/EAN: 9783337733926

Printed in Europe, USA, Canada, Australia, Japan

Cover: Foto ©Raphael Reischuk / pixelio.de

More available books at **www.hansebooks.com**

HISTORICAL SKETCH

OF

Major JOSEPH HAWLEY

OF NORTHAMPTON, MASS.

1723—1788

A REPRINT FROM THE

"HAWLEY RECORD"

1300— 1890

**For a detailed description of the HAWLEY RECORD
see fly-leaf at the end of this Sketch**

BUFFALO, N. Y.

1890

SKETCH.

Note 230.—MAJOR JOSEPH HAWLEY, A.M., No. 6222, son of Lieut. Joseph and Rebecca (Stoddard) Hawley, of Northampton, Mass., was born 8 Oct., 1723, and graduated at Yale College in 1742, a little before he was nineteen years of age; studied law and established himself in his profession in his native town, where he was Town Clerk in 1749, and a Justice of the Peace in 1752, when he married Mercy, daughter of Joseph and Abigail (Lewis) Lyman. They had no children, but brought up a boy named Joseph Hawley Clarke, who died at Springfield, Mass. (For the Lyman family, see Note 126.)

The monument to the memory of Mr. Hawley is in the form of an old fashioned table about three feet high, and four feet long by three wide. The inscription reads:

THIS MONUMENT
ERECTED BY JOSEPH CLARKE
TO THE MEMORY OF THE
HON. JOSEPH HAWLEY, Esqr.,
WHO DIED MARCH 10TH, 1788,
AGED 64 YEARS.

"On the 21st of March, 1759, the Indians appeared at Colrain [Eastern Vermont] and captured John McConn and his wife. The latter was sacrificed to the early cruelty of her captors on the second day's march. A party of militia, led by Major Hawley of Northampton, started in pursuit, but the enemy were soon at a safe distance, and the troops proceeded no further than Greenfield." (Hist. Vermont, p. 88.)

It appears that thus early Mr. Hawley held a military title, and by it he was always known. He afterwards refused all offers of higher titles, and public offices except Representative.

In 1740 an Association of merchants and others, of Boston and vicinity, was formed to furnish a currency for the benefit of trade and business in general, then greatly depressed by lack of a circulating medium. This institution was called " the Land Bank, or Manufactory Scheme." This " Scheme," after a considerable issue of bills, failed, or rather was suppressed by English authority. In connection with some of the transactions of this Association, the following poetic effusion was discovered and published.* It is here produced because of the high compliment to Maj. Joseph Hawley of Northampton, with others, as being incapable of being turned from rectitude of character under any circumstances.

> " When Major Hawley goes astray,
> And Otis knows not what to say ;
> When Gen'ral Ruggles falsehood speaks,
> And Sampson Stoddard silence keeps ;
> When Col'nel Cotton wins his wager,
> And Father Witt is made a major ;
> When Col'nel Noyes shall keep his seat,
> Land Banks shall be no more a cheat."

* N. E. Hist. and Genealogical Register, vol. xiv., 263.

5

5

History claims great things for herself, and is, perhaps, entitled to a degree of praise for what she tells us about the past; but the facts she does *not* record, and the characters she wholly neglects and ignores, are a thousand to one to those she mentions. Voluminous as are the records of other times, we should consider them stinted and imperfect indeed, could we see at a glance the unrecorded great events which have transpired, and the unnamed and unknown great characters who have lived on the earth.

It is not an uncommon occurrence that men largely instrumental in producing great and beneficent changes in public affairs "get left," as the phrase is, when history makes up its record. Some accident, some false impression, some oversight or prejudice, some personal bias—modesty, false or true, one side, or brazen cheek on the other, contrives to leave in obscurity a truly worthy name, while another, less worthy, or worthy not at all, is lifted above the horizon, and as years pass, is taken more and more distinctly as the proper representative of an era or an idea.

One of the most praiseworthy employments, therefore, of the historic press and of historical societies, is to rescue from threatened oblivion such important facts and such deserving characters before they are beyond human reach down the ever-rolling river.

Letter of Hon. Charles Francis Adams.

QUINCY, MASS., 8 October, 1848.

Elias S. Hawley, Esq., Buffalo:

DEAR SIR : It has always been to me a matter of serious regret that so little remains of the personal history of Major Hawley. What appears of his action during the Revolution has given me a very exalted notion of his character, yet so far as I know, the little tribute paid to his memory in Mr. Tudor's Life of Otis, is the only one now to be found. This ought not to be. I am therefore glad to understand from your letter that you are about to give us something additional. I wish I could help you more, but if nothing else you have my good wishes at least.

The letter to which you refer is not extant so far as I can ascertain. I have of Major Hawley's handwriting only two remnants, one of them a brief note addressed to Mrs. A. Adams, my grandmother, requesting a loan of a law book. The other, a very interesting letter to John Adams, pointing out the policy to be adopted by the Massachusetts delegates in the first congress. Of this letter I will furnish you a copy, if you desire it. It has never been printed.*

All that I know besides, of Major Hawley, is to be found in the journals of the Provincial Congress, which were printed in 1838, and in the late volumes of the American Archives, published by Mr. Force, at Washington. These afford proof of the vigour of his character, and of the great influence which he exercised in the councils of the Patriot Provincial Congress. That he allowed a false delicacy to limit the sphere of his usefulness is the only indication of weakness that I find. Mr. Tudor says of him, that the imputation of selfish views was so insupportable to him, he resolved never to accept of any office whatever. If General Washington and the other patriots of the Revolution had followed such a rule of action, what would have become of the country? Had Major Hawley fol-

* See fac-simile of the first and copy of the second of the letters here mentioned, on pages 8 and 9.

lowed a different system, he would unquestionably have been a very efficient leader in the Congress of the confederation where they very often wanted just such a person, and his name and influence would have remained much more strongly impressed upon the younger generations in Massachusetts than now. The opinion upon which he acted is not uncommon among a very honest and independent class of our citizens, to wit: that the power of affixing a suspicion of wrong motive must be taken away from opponents at all hazards, be it even to the abnegation of the means of extensive usefulness. The foundation of it is fear of unjust censure, a motive which I cannot very highly appreciate. Neither does it seem to me entirely in keeping with the other portion of Major Hawley's character as we see it in the few letters he has left. I therefore hope that in this particular Mr. Tudor may have somewhat misconceived it, and that some other cause operated to prevent him from pursuing the entire career which at one time lay open to him.

I do not know how I got it, but the impression is strong in my mind that the selection of the first delegates to the Federal Congress in 1774, and particularly the nomination of my grandfather, was very much the act of Major Hawley. That he was the guiding spirit in the centre of the province during the whole critical period of transition from colonial to free government is unquestionable. I hope you may find material enough to make the fact fully to appear in the eyes of posterity.

Very respectfully,

Your obd't serv't,

CHARLES FRANCIS ADAMS.

Watertown 23 Sept 1775

Mrs Adams

The Publick have great need of two Vols. of Mr Adams English Statutes at large — The edition which Mr Adams owns is (if I don't mistake) Ruffhead's The one Vol. which is wanted is that which contains the Statutes of 27th of Edward the Third and the other which is Needed contains the Statutes of the 23d of Henry ye 8th —

I would not ask such a favour Madam, if the publick was not made interested — I shall desire Col Thayer to be particularly careful in bringing them — after their arrival — I will undertake that they be most carefully used and will be responsible for ye speedy return of them — I don't know where else they can be obtain'd —

I am madm Your most respectful and Obedient Sert

Joseph Hawley

Major Joseph Hawley to John Adams.

NORTHAMPTON, 25 July, 1774.

DEAR SIR: I never received nor heard of your letter of the 27th June last wrote at Ipswich until the 22d instant. Immediately on the receipt of it I set myself to consider of an answer to it. What I first remark is your great distrust of your abilities for the service assigned you. However I say that I imagine that I have some knowledge of your abilities, and I assure you Sir, I gave my vote for you most heartily, and I have not yet repented of it. My opinion is that our Committee taken together is the best we could have taken in the province. I should be extremely sorry that any one of them should fail of going: the absence of any one of them will destroy that happy balance or equilibrium which they will form together. I acknowledge that the service is most important and I don't know who is fully equal to it, the importance of the business ought not to beget despondency in any one, but to excite to the greatest circumspection the most attentive and mature consideration and calmest deliberation, courage and fortitude must be maintained. If we give way to despondency it will soon be all over with us; rashness must be avoided; the end or effect of every measure proposed must be thoroughly contemplated before it be adopted. It must be well looked to that the measure be feasible and practicable. If we make attemptes and fail in them, Lord North will call them impudent and futile and the Tories will triumph.

It appears to me, sir, that the congress ought first to settle with absolute precission the object or objects to be pursued as whether the end of all shall be the repeal of the tea duty only, or that and the molasses duty, or them and opening the port of Boston or them and also the restoration of the Charter of Massachusetts Bay (for it is easy to demonstrate that the late act for regulation &c. in its effects annuls the whole Charter, so far as the Charter granted any privilege). When the objects or ends to be pursued are clearly and certainly settled, the means or measures to be used to obtain and effect those ends can be better judged of, most certainly the objects must be definitely agreed on, and settled by the Congress first or last.

As to means and measures I am not fully settled or determined in my own mind. It may not be prudent fully to explain myself in writing upon that head; the letter may miscarry.

You are pleased to say that extremities and ruptures, it is our policy to avoid. I agree if any other means will answer our ends, or if it is plain they would not.

But let me say, sir, that with me it is settled as a maxim and first truth—that the people, or State who will not or cannot defend their liberties and rights will not have any for any long time, they will be Slaves. Some other State will find them out and will subjugate them.

You say, Sir, that measures to check and interrupt the torrent of luxury are most agreeable to your sentiments. Pray Sir, did any thing ever do it but necessity?

The institution of annual congresses, you suppose will brighten the chain and would make excellent statesmen and politicians. I agree it; but pray Sir, don't you imagine that such an institution would breed *extremities* and *ruptures?* It appears to me most clear that the institution if formed must be discontinued or we must defend it with ruptures.

I suggested above that my letter might miscarry, and we don't know when we write to what hands our letters may come. I should therefore be extremely glad to see some or all of the committee as they pass through this county. If there were any hopes of obtaining the favor I would beg them all to come through Northampton ; it would not be more than twenty miles farther and as good a road. But I imagine they will all pass through Springfield ; and the favor I earnestly ask of you Sir, is that you would be pleased to inform me by letter by our post, on what day you expect to be at Springfield—and I will endeavor to see the Committee there altho' I should wait there two or three days for it. Pray Sir, don't fail of sending me this intelligence—you will probably receive this letter on Saturday this week by Mr. Wilde our Post he keeps Sabbath at Boston he commonly comes out on Monday about eleven o'clock. You may find him—or if you have a letter for him to take either at Messrs. Edes & Gills office or at Mersrs. Fleets in the forenoon it will probably come safe to me next week on Wednesday. I will prevail with him (if I can) to call on you to take a line from you for me. Information of the time you intend to be at Springfield, I am very anxious to obtain. Pray sir, oblige me with it.

But as it is possible that I may miss of seeing the committee or any of them, which will indeed be to me a very great disappointment, I ask leave to make myself free enough to suggest the following which if you judge proper I consent you should communicate to your Brethren : you can't Sir, but be fully apprised that a good issue of the congress depends a good deal on the harmony, good understanding, and I had almost said brotherly love of its members, and everything tending to beget and improve such mutual affections, and indeed to cement the body ought to be practised, and everything in the least tending to create disgust or strangeness coldness or so much as indifference carefully avoided. Now there is an opinion which does in some degree obtain in the other colonies that the Massachusetts gentlemen and especially of the town of Boston do affect to dictate and take the lead in continental measures; that we are apt from an inward vanity and self-conceit to assume big and haughty airs. Whether this opinion has any foundation in fact, I am not certain. Our own tories propogate it if they did not at first suggest it Now I pray that everything in the conduct and behavior of our gentlemen which might tend to beget and strengthen such an opinion might be most carefully avoided. It is highly probable in my opinion that you will meet Gentlemen from several of the other colonies fully equal to yourselves, or any of you in their knowledge of Great Britain, the Colonies, Law, History, Government, Commerce &c. I know some of the gentlemen from Connecticut are very sensible, ingenuous, solid men— who will go from New York I have not heard, but I know there are very able men there and by what we from time to time see in the public papers, and what our assembly and committees have received from the assemblies and committees of the more southern colonies we must be satisfied that they have men of as much sense and literature as any we can or ever could boast of. But enough of this sort and I ask pardon that I have said so much of it.

Another thing I beg leave just to hint, that it is very likely you may meet divers gentlemen in Congress who are of Dutch or Scotch or Irish extract—many more there are in those Southern Colonies of those descents, than in these New England Colonies, and many of them very worthy, learned men Query therefore whether prudence would not direct that everything should be very cautiously avoided which could give the least umbrage, disgust or affront to any of such pedigree; for as "of every nation and blood he that feareth God and worketh righteousness is accepted of Him," so they ought to be of us. Small things may have important effects in such a business; that which disparages our family ancestors or nation is apt to stick by us, if cast up in Company, and their blood you will find is as warm as ours.

One thing I want that the Southern Gentlemen should be deeply impressed with that is that all acts of British Legislation which influence and affect our internal polity, are as absolutely repugnant to Liberty and the idea of our being a free people as Taxation or Revenue Acts. Witness the present Regulation act for this province, and if we should not be subdued by what is done already, like acts will undoubtedly be made for other Colonies. I expect nothing but new Treasons, new Felonies, new Misprisions, new Praemunires, & not to say the Lord, the Devil knows what.

Pray Sir, let Mr. Samuel Adams know that our top tories here give out most confidently that he will certainly be took up before the Congress. I am timid not with regard to myself and friend, but I am satisfied that they have such advice from head quarters. Please to give my hearty regards to him, the speaker & all the gentlemen of the Congress, and I beg neither of them would on any account make default, if they do there will be great searching of heart. You may all manage the journey so that it will be pleasant and very much serve your health, and that God would bless you all, is the most fervent prayer of

Sir, your hearty friend and most obedient servant,

JOSEPH HAWLEY.

Pray Sir don't fail of acquainting me when you shall be in our county.   J. H.

Extracts from Tudor's "Life of Otis," p. 253.

"JOSEPH HAWLEY, JOHN HANCOCK, SAMUEL ADAMS.

"The Legislature of this year (1766) received an accession of three eminent members, who were returned to it for the first time : Joseph Hawley, John Hancock, and Samuel Adams.

"Major Hawley, a representative from Northampton, acquired a very remarkable influence in the public councils. Perhaps Massachusetts can boast of no citizen in all her annals, more estimable. He continued in the legislature till 1776, and during that period it has been said, that no vote on any public measure, either was or could have been carried without his assent.

"Joseph Hawley was born in 1723, educated at Yale College in 1742, and followed the profession of the law at Northampton, where he died in 1788, aged 64 years. As a lawyer he was possessed of great learning; able as a reasoner, and a very manly, impressive speaker. He was at the head of the bar in the western counties of the Province; he had studied with diligence the principles of law as connected with political institutions. This had prepared him for a clear perception of the effects that would have resulted from the execution of the ministerial plans against the colonies; and caused him to take the most ardent and decisive part against the Stamp Act, and the whole series of arbitrary measures that followed it. The adherents of the administration dreaded him more than any individual in his part of the country, and as usual, endeavored though most completely in vain, to injure his character. They succeeded indeed, in three official persecutions, in throwing him over the bar, to which he was however soon restored.

"The almost unexampled influence acquired by Major Hawley was owing not only to his great talents, but still more perhaps to his highminded, unsullied, unimpeachable integrity. His enemies sought to undermine his reputation by calumniating his motives, as was their manner toward every distinguished man on the patriotic side. They said, his conduct was factious and principally ruinous, and that the only object which he and his coadjutors of Massachusetts had in view was to bring themselves into power under a new order of things. The imputation of selfish, sordid views was insupportable to a man of his character. He therefore at once resolved, and pledged himself never to accept any promotion, office or emolument under any government. This pledge he severely redeemed. He refused even all promotion in the militia, was several times chosen a Counsellor, but declined; and would accept of no other public trust than the nearly gratuitous one of representing his town. A modest estate which descended to him from his father [a] and uncle, was adequate to support his plain style of living, and he had no desire to accumulate wealth. His character was so noble and consistent, that his fellow citizens reposed unhesitating confidence in his integrity; they believed that all the honours and wealth of the mother country would be insufficient to corrupt him, and while they saw daily that he sought nothing from his own party. His talents, judgment, and firmness came in aid of this reputation for disinterestedness, and gave him on all occasions the power of an umpire. The weight of his character was sufficient to balance all the interest, which several gentlemen of great respectability in the western counties exerted in favor of the administration. The country members espe followed his opinions implicitly, and the most powerful in the Legislature would probably have been unsuccessful, if they had attempted to carry any measure against his opinion.

"The ascendancy which was allotted him by the deference of others, was a fortunate circumstance for his country. Never was influence exercised with more singleness of heart, with more intelligent, devoted and inflexible patriotism. He made up his mind earlier than most men, that the struggle against oppression would lead to war, and that our rights at last must be secured by our arms. As the crisis approached, when some persons urged upon him the danger of a contest so apparently unequal, his answer was, ' We must put to sea ; Providence will bring us into port.' [b]

" Major Hawley did not appear in the Legislature after the year 1776, but he never relaxed his zeal in service of his country, and was always ready to contribute his efforts to the public service. By his private exertions, he rendered assistance at some very critical and discouraging periods. At the season when the prospects of the American army were most gloomy, when the Jerseys were overrun, and the feelings of many were on the verge of despondency, he exerted himself with great activity and success to rally the spirits of his fellow citizens. At this time, when apathy appeared stealing upon the country, and the people were reluctant to march on a seemingly desperate service, he addressed a body of militia, to urge them to volunteer as recruits. His manly eloquence, his powerful appeals to their pride, their patriotism, their duty, to everything which they held dear and sacred, awakened their dormant feelings, and ev ited them to enthusiasm [c]

On another occasion he rendered a service of much higher , and may be said not only to have prevented, but to have radically destroyed an incipient insurrection. At a time when the burthens and distress of the war had produced great discontent, and even disaffection in some quarters, and Samuel Ely, a notorious demagogue, had by his factious and treasonable efforts gone far to organize in the western part of the State an almost open resistance to the government, delegates from a large number of towns met in convention at Hatfield. The Legislature sent Messrs. Samuel Adams, Stephen Gorham, and General Ward, as commissioners to meet them, and avert if possible the threatened danger. It was a moment of peril and anxiety. Major Hawley was a delegate from Northampton. At the opening of the meeting, the elements of mischief were visible in all their malignity, and seemed ready to burst into open fury. Hawley, with the deepest solicitude, which in great minds is the certain foundation of coolness and self-possession, addressed this convention, consisting of two hundred. His spotless and lofty integrity, before which even the most callous demagogues shrunk abashed, prepared the way to that triumph which his masterly talents achieved. Argument, satire, pleasantry, alternate appeals to their passions and to their reason, all managed with consummate address and invincible energy, gradually subdued their inflamed, refractory humour, and finally moulded them entirely to his will. They not only renounced all their dangerous intentions, but agreed to sign a humble petition to the government, promising future obedience and praying for an act of indemnity for the past, and to make the victory more complete, and to show the danger was entirely destroyed, they were brought with the exception of five persons, to sign the petition, excluding Ely, the leader of all the disturbance, from the indemnity. [d]

"Major Hawley was a sincerely religious and pious man ; but here as in politics, he loathed all tyranny and fanatical usurpation. He was, near the close of his life, chosen into the Senate of Massachusetts. Though he would not have taken the trust at any rate, he seized the opportunity to give his testimony against the test act, which to a recent period was a stain in the constitution of that State. In a letter upon the subject, he asked if it was necessary that he should be called upon to renounce the authority of the King of Great Britain and every foreign potentate? and whether it could be expected that, having been a member of the church for forty years, he should submit to the insult of being called to swear that he believed in the truth of the Christian religion before he could take his seat?*

"With all these powerful talents and noble feelings, he was not exempt from misfortune, that occasionally threw its dark shadows over him. He was subject at particular times to an hypocondriac disorder, that would envelope him in gloom and despondency. At these seasons he was oppressed with melancholy, and would lament every action and exertion of his life. When his mind recovered its tone, the recollection of these sufferings was painful and he disliked to have them remembered.

"Major Hawley was a patriot without personal animosities, an orator without vanity, a lawyer without chicanery, a gentleman without ostentation, a statesman without duplicity, and a Christian without bigotry. As a man of commanding

* The test was copied almost verbatim from the English test act, and its insertion in the liberal constitution of Massachusetts was a mortifying anomaly. At a late revision of that instrument, by a general convention, this remnant of superannuated bigotry was expunged by general consent.

talents, his firm renunciation and self-denial of all ambitious
views would have secured him that respect which such strength
of mind inevitably inspires, while his voluntary and zealous
devotion to the service of his countrymen established him in
their affection. His uprightness and plainness united to his
ability and disinterestedness, gave the most extensive influence
to his opinions, and in a period of doubt, division and danger,
men sought relief from their perplexities in his authority, and
suffered their course to be guided by him when they distrusted
their own judgments or the counsel of others. He, in fine,
formed one of those manly, public-spirited and generous citizens, ready to share peril and decline reward, who illustrate the
idea of a commonwealth, and who, through the obstructions of
human passions and infirmities, being of rare occurrence, will
always be the most admired, appropriate, noble ornaments of a
free government."

In the same work at page 248 Mr. Tudor says :

" The answer of this House [to a communication of Sir F.
Bernard] was made by a committee composed of Mr. Cushing,
the Speaker, of course according to the practice of that day,
Otis, Major Hawley, Mr. Samuel Adams, Mr. Landers, Colonel
O. Partridge and Col. Bowers. Generally speaking, the first
three gentlemen, after the speaker, were on all political committees, and also Mr. Hancock. Otis was the chairman, and his
zeal, learning and readiness were all in requisition for draught-
ing reports ; these were afterwards a little moderated by Cushing, revised and polished by Adams, and decided upon by Maj.
Hawley, if necessary, whose opinion and influence were all-
powerful in the Legislature.

Again at page 279 :

" They [the House] assembled again December 3d, and passed the bill for granting ' compensation to the sufferers, and general pardon, indemnity and oblivion to the offenders ' (in the Stamp Act Riots). The members were divided, 53 to 35. Otis, Adams, Hancock, Hawley, etc., being in the affirmative. The House ordered that Major Hawley, Mr. Otis, and Mr. Adams be a committee to prepare a resolve, setting forth the motives which induced this House to pass the Bill for granting compensation, etc., etc., who reported thereon as follows :" [Here follows the report.]

Again at page 292 :

" The speech of the Governor at the opening of the winter session in 1768, merely related to some boundary line between this province and some of the adjoining ones. The House soon appointed a committee to take into consideration the situation of public affairs. The number and names of this committee will show how much importance was attached to their deliberations. It consisted of the speaker (Mr. Cushing), Colonel Otis, Mr. Adams, Major Hawley, Mr. Otis, Mr. Hancock, Capt. Sheaffe, Colonel Bowers and Mr. Dexter."

Again at page 312 :

" In looking back to this period (the presentation of ' a series of petitions and remonstrances, friendly and respectful indeed, but most earnest, urgent and unanswerable'), the blind arrogance, indifference or ignorance of the British Councils respecting American affairs, seems almost incredible. What must have been the feelings of such men as Otis, Hawley, Adams, Hancock, Cushing, Dexter and others on receiving, while in breathless expectation, the assurance that 'the time was not proper' to present their petition ! the gentlemen were too much heated by electioneering disputes to 'pay attention to America,' but he (the agent) would 'watch for an opportunity to throw in their petitions'! How must these men, absorbed in patriotic anxieties, standing on the portentous verge to which they were driven, have read such a communication ! with what bitter mortification, what alienating disgust, must they have heard such pretences and excuses for disregarding all their instant appeals and entreaties ! How must the inevitable resort to independence for self-preservation, have rushed upon their minds ! how vividly they must have foreseen the alternative, that after a few more petitions, remonstrances, and resolutions, 'AFTER ALL, THEY MUST FIGHT.' "

Again at page 342 :

[The House having requested the Governor, at the session commencing the last Wednesday of May, 1769, to remove the armed force " by sea and land out of this port and the gates of this city during this session," etc., etc.,] " The answer of the Governor was laconic : ' Gentlemen, I have no authority over his majesty's ships in this port, or his troops in this town; nor can I give any orders for the removal of the same.' Otis and his father, who had been again negatived as a Counsellor, together with Hawley, Hancock, Adams, Puble and Warren, were the committee for answering this speech. They began by declaring," etc.

Again at page 349 :

" Governor Barnard having sent messages on the 6th and 12th July (1769), on the subject of providing funds to discharge the expense of quartering the troops in Boston, [e] an answer was made by a committee composed of nearly the same individuals as many previous ones which have been mentioned—Colonel Otis, Major Hawley, Col. Williams, Mr. Adams, Mr. Otis, Col. Ward and Mr. Hancock. The conclusion of this message, the last which the House sent to Governor Barnard, is both for style and matter, such as might be expected from the men who prepared it. ' We shall now with your Excellency's leave,' " etc.

Again at page 370 :

"The Legislature having met at Cambridge, March 15, 1770, an answer was made to a message of the Lieut. Governor ' in which he called their attention to a disturbance that had taken place in the town of Gloucester.' This answer will be found in the Massachusetts State Papers, p. 203. The Committee were Col. Otis, Mr. Williams of Taunton, Maj. Hawley, Mr. S. Adams, Mr. Otis, Mr. Hancock and Mr. Saunders of Gloucester." [f]

Again at page 406, chap. xxv. and onward :

" Though Otis was not a member of the Legislature after 1771,[g] and the motive of giving a sketch of legislative proceedings connected with him has ceased, yet there was one occurrence in 1773, that was of too much consequence to be passed over without at least a slight notice, as it furnished material of the highest value and interest to the Historian, and to every civilian who wishes to investigate the original relations of the English and Colonial governments.

" At the winter session, 1773, Governor Hutchinson, in his speech to the Legislature" attempted to show that the happiness and prosperity of the colonies depended on the continuance of their connection with the parent state. "He invited them to discuss the subject, and challenged them to overthrow the principles that he laid down, to which he thought they must accede, or else claim independence, 'which' he said, 'I cannot allow to think you have in contemplation.' The answer of the House is a profoundly learned and elaborate exposition of the rights of the colonists, under the constitution and the charter, and confutes the whole argument of the Governor. Three weeks afterward, the Governor delivered a long rejoinder and proved ' that he could argue still. ' To this speech the council made a short answer; but the House, notwithstanding the regrets which they expressed at the consideration of the questions, showed themselves not loth to continue their refutation. Their reply is even more extended than the former one, descending into some minute details, and proceeding with a more emphatic tone to deny the supremacy of parliament. *The first plain avowal of independence* by any legislative body in the colonies is to be found in these answers of the house of representatives.

"The speeches and answers that have been alluded to, will be found in the Massachusetts State Papers, from p. 336 to 399. These answers were written by President Adams, though his name does not appear among the committee, as he was not a member of the Legislature. This circumstance was owing to Major Hawley, who proposed to his colleagues that Mr. Adams should be called to join in their conferences; because as Hutchinson had thrown the gauntlet in a very laboured production, it was necessary to use great precaution in answering him. The draught prepared by President Adams was accepted by the committee unanimously."

Again at page 461, in speaking of General Warren, Mr. Tudor says :

" He was one of those persons who saw very early ' *that we must fight*,' and the impetuosity of a young and gallant spirit made him always ready for the alternative."

Notes to the Extracts from Tudor.

[*a*] "Joseph Hawley settled in Northampton in 1677, was the son of Thomas Hawley of Roxbury. He was educated at Harvard College. He died in 1711. His children were Lydia, born 1680; Joseph, 1682; Dorothy, 1684; Samuel, 1686; Thomas, 1689; Ebenezer, 1694. Of these four sons, Joseph lived in Northampton; Samuel settled in Hadley or Amherst, where some of his posterity remain; Thomas settled in Ridgefield, Connecticut; Ebenezer lived in Northampton and had no children.

"Joseph Hawley, son of Joseph, who died in 1735, had two children : Joseph, born 1723, and Elisha, born 1726. Elisha was slain in the battle near Lake George, Sept. 8, 1755. He left no children. His brother Joseph was the distinguished Major Hawley, a patriot of the Revolution, &c. He died childless in 1788, and the race came to an end in Northampton."

(MS. Letter from Sylvester Judd, Northampton, Mass., 27 Feb., 1845, to E. S. Hawley.)

[*b*] The following, taken from a letter of President John Adams to Mr. Wirt, is highly characteristic of Mr. Hawley and also contains some very interesting notices of other eminent individuals :

"When congress had finished their business," says Mr. Adams, "in the autumn of 1774, I had with Mr. Henry, before

we took leave of each other, some familiar conversation, in which
I expressed a full conviction that our resolves, declarations of
rights, enumerations of wrongs, petitions, remonstrances and ad-
dresses, associations and non-importation agreements, however
they might be respected in America, and however necessary to
cement the union of the colonies, would be but waste water in
England. Mr. Henry said they might make some impression
among the people of England, but agreed with me that they
would be totally lost upon the government. I had but just received a short and hasty letter, written to me by Major Joseph
Hawley of Northampton, containing 'A Few Broken Hints,' as
he called them, of what he thought was proper to be done, and
concluding with the words, 'after all we must fight.'

"This letter I read to Mr. Henry, who listened with
great attention, and as soon as I had pronounced the words,
'After all, we must fight,' he raised his head with an energy
and vehemence that I can never forget, and broke out with 'By
God, I am of that man's mind.' I put the letter into his hand,
and when he had read it he returned it to me with an
equally solemn asseveration that he agreed entirely in the opinion of the writer. I considered this a sacred oath upon a very
great occasion (and would have sworn it as religiously as he did),
and by no means inconsistent with what you say, in some part
of your book, that he never took the sacred name in vain.

"As I knew the sentiments with which Mr. Henry left Congress in 1774, and knew the chapter and verse from which he
had borrowed the sublime expression, 'We must fight,' I was
not at all surprised at your history in the 122d page [In Wirt's
"Life of Patrick Henry," at page 122, Mr. W. reports Mr. Henry's
speech (in part) on his famous Virginia Resolutions, and sub-

joins a note as follows: "There is no longer any room for hope. If we wish to be free—if we wish to preserve inviolate those inestimable privileges for which we have been so long contending—if we mean not basely to abandon the noble struggle in which we have been so long engaged and which we pledged ourselves never to abandon, until the glorious object of our contest shall be obtained—we must fight!—I repeat it, sir, we must fight!! An appeal to arms and to the God of Hosts is all that is left us." "Imagine to yourself," says my correspondent (Judge Tucker) "this sentence delivered with all the calm dignity of Cato of Utica—imagine to yourself the Roman Senate assembled in the Capitol, when it was entered by the profane Gauls, who at first were awed by their presence, as if they had entered an assembly of the gods!—imagine that you heard that Cato addressing such a Senate—imagine that you saw the handwriting on the wall in Belshazzar's palace—imagine you heard a voice as from heaven uttering the words, ' We must fight,' as the doom of fate, and you may have some idea of the speaker, the assembly to whom he addressed himself, and the auditory, of which I was one."] in the note and in some of the preceding and following pages. Mr. Henry only pursued in March, 1775, the views and vows of 1774.

"The other delegates from Virginia returned to their State in full confidence that all our grievances would be redressed. The last words that Mr. Richard Henry, Sr., said to me when we parted, were : 'We shall infallibly carry all our points. You will be completely relieved; all the offensive acts will be repealed; the army and fleet will be recalled, and Britain will give up her foolish project.'

"Washington only was in doubt. He never spoke in public.

In private he joined with those who advocated a non-exporta-
tion, as well as a non-importation agreement. With both, he
thought we should prevail; without either he thought it doubt-
ful. Henry was clear in one opinion; Richard Henry, Sr., in
an opposite opinion; and Washington doubted between the two.
Henry, however, appeared in the end to be exactly right."

In the "Life and Writings of Washington," by Jared
Sparks, vol. 2, p. 405, occurs a letter written by John Augustin
Washington to his brother George, to which is appended the
following note on the same page, dated Richmond, 25 March,
1775:

"Washington was now attending the second Virginia Convention, which met at Richmond on the 20th of March. At
this convention Patrick Henry introduced resolutions for putting
the colony in a state of defence, and embodying arming and dis-
ciplining a sufficient number of men for that purpose. This was
considered a bold measure and was opposed by some of the ab-
lest patriots in the assembly. It was on this occasion and in defense of his resolutions, that Mr. Henry uttered his memorable
declaration, 'We must fight! I repeat it, sir, we must fight! An
appeal to arms and the God of Hosts is all that is left to us.'
The resolutions were carried and a plan adopted for putting
them in execution. Washington was one of the committee for
drafting and reporting the plan.

"In connexion with the above declaration of Patrick
Henry, it is proper to state that the expression 'We must fight'
was used four months previously by the ardent patriot Major
Hawley of Massachusetts in a letter to Mr. John Adams, which
Mr. Adams showed to Mr. Henry while they were together in the
first congress. (Tudor's 'Life of Otis,' page 256.)"

[c] In the "Life and Writings of Washington," by Sparks, vol. iii. p. 437, occurs a letter, dated New York, June 24, 1776, from Maj. Gen. Scuyler to Washington, on the subject of the militia, to a part of which is appended the following note, viz :

"The following extract from a letter written to Washington by the ardent and patriotic Joseph Hawley, of Massachusetts, June 21st, relating to the proposed reinforcements of militia, is characteristic of the author:

"'The most important matters are soon to be decided by arms. Unhappy it is for the Massachusetts, and I fear, for the whole continent, that at this season we have a numerous assembly. More than one-half the house are new members. Their decisions are most afflictingly slow, when everything calls for the utmost ardor and dispatch. The Lord have mercy upon us! This colony, I imagine will raise the men required by Congress, before snow falls, but in no season for the relief of either New York or Canada. Pray Sir, consider what there is to be done. It is my clear opinion, that there will not a single company move in this colony for either of those places these three weeks. I know Sir, it will vex you, but you will not be alone in the vexation. My soul at times, is ready to die within me, at others my blood to press out at the pores of my body. But what shall be the expedients? I never was good at them. If I may say it, I am astonished at the policy of Congress in ordering more regiments here, instead of ordering those which are here, to parts where they are infinitely more needed; but my opinion is little worth. Such as it is, I have given it.'

"Again Mr. Hawley pressed this subject, on the 27th of June, and added : 'For God's sake, if it is possible, let all

Ward's people be instantly ordered to Canada, or to some place where they are more needed than here. Pray, Sir, consider that they are officered, armed and equipped in all respects. Everything is to be done for the militia. Our people will fight here *pro aris et focis:* but very few of them, believe me, will be got to Canada this year. I pray your Excellency's pardon for my troublesome repetition of this matter to you. I am here and see the true state and posture of affairs. No place on the continent I conceive is more secure than Boston.'"

[d] To show that the influence exerted by Major Hawley was not confined either to the militia, the popular assembly or the hall of Legislation alone, it is sufficient to adduce the following extract from Sparks' "Life of Washington," vol. iii. p. 488, Appendix. After giving a tabular view of the army :

"An army thus constituted could hardly contain within itself the elements of uniformity or discipline. There was in reality no other bond of union than voluntary acquiescence, and no controlling head vested with any adequate power to maintain authority. By common consent Massachusetts was allowed to take the lead. Not only the usual affairs of the army were administered by General Ward, but courts-martial were held by his order, and punishments inflicted. Experience had proved, however, that the officers were deficient in the requisite qualifications for the rank they sustained, which is not surprising, when it is considered upon what principle the Massachusetts had been commissioned. Several arrests and trials had taken place for misconduct or cowardice, even at the memorable action of Bunker Hill. Two days after he arrived in Cambridge (to take command of the army), Washington received the following impressive letter on this subject, from Joseph Hawley, then a member of the Massachusetts Provincial Congress :

" ' WATERTOWN, 5 July, 1775.
" ' SIR :

" ' You were pleased the other day to mention to Col. Warren and me as your opinion, that it was highly probable Gage's troops would very shortly attack our army in some part or other. I believe your opinion is not ill founded, and I am sure your Excellency will be pleased with every intimation, that may in any degree aid you in the choice of measures tending to success and victory. Therefore, that I may not be tedious, I ask your pardon when I suggest, that although in the Massachusetts part of the army, there are divers brave and intrepid officers, yet there are too many, and even several colonels, whose characters, to say the least, are very equivocal with respect to courage. There is much more cause to fear that the officers will fail in a day of trial, than the privates. I may venture to say, that if the officers will do their duty, there is no fear of the soldiery.

" ' I therefore most humbly propose to your consideration, the propriety and advantage of your making immediately a most solemn and peremptory declaration, to all the officers of the army, in general orders or otherwise as your wisdom shall direct, assuring them that every officer, who in the Day of Battle shall fully do his duty, shall not fail of your kindest notices and highest marks of your favour : but on the other hand, that every officer, who on such a day shall act the poltroon, dishonour his General, and by failing of his duty, betray his country, shall infallibly meet his deserts, whatever his rank, connexions or interests may be, and that no intercessions on his behalf will be likely to be of any avail for his pardon.

"' I know that your Excellency is able to form a declaration of the kind conceived in such style, and replete with such determined sentiments and spirit, as cannot fail of begetting a full belief and persuasion in the hearts of such to whom it shall be addressed, that the same will be infallibly executed. I am almost certain the measure will have the happiest tendency. *Sed sapienti verbum sat est.*

"' Pray pardon my prolixity. I never was happy enough to be concise. I am, with the greatest respect and deference, your Excellency's most obedient, humble servant,

JOSEPH HAWLEY.

"'To General Washington.'

" It was no doubt in consequence of this suggestion and advice, that the following order was issued on the 7th of July, after approving the decision of the Court in the case of Captain John Callender:

"'The General having made all due inquiries and maturely considered this matter, is led to the above determination, not only from the particular guilt of Captain Callender but the fatal consequences of such conduct to the army, and the cause of America. He now, therefore, most earnestly exhorts officers of all ranks to show an example of bravery and courage to their men, assuring them, that such as do their duty in the day of Battle, as brave and good officers, shall be honored with every mark of distinction and regard, and their names and merits be made known to the General Congress and all America; while on the other hand, he positively declares, that every officer, be his rank what it may, who shall betray his country, and dishonor the army and his General, by basely keeping back and shrinking from his duty in any engagement, shall be held up

as an infamous coward, and punished as such with the utmost
martial severity ; and no connexions, interest, or intercessions
in his behalf will avail to prevent the strict execution of
justice.' "

(e) " 1769. Although acts for taxes were pronounced null,
yet the general authority of Parliament over the colonies had
not been denied; but, in some of the pamphlets which were
brought to America, it was now advanced that the King by his
representative, the Governor, with the council and the house of
representatives in each colony, constitute a full and sole legislative power, and consequently the legislative power of parliament must be excluded. In Massachusetts Bay, a representative of one of the towns of the county of Hampshire, an eminent lawyer and highly esteemed [in . note, "Joseph Hawley,
Esq.,"] made a public declaration in the house, that he knew
not how parliament could have acquired a right of legislation
over the colonies. In a public town meeting of the inhabitants
of Boston, a motion was made, and exceptions being taken to
it, because it implied a general independency upon parliament,
one of the representatives of the town [in note, " Mr. Samuel
Adams "] undertook to obviate the exception, and concluded in
this manner: 'Independent we are, and independent we
will be.'

" At first these were said to be bold strokes, and were not
pleasing to the greatest part of the people. The newspaper
writers soon availed themselves of such examples, and the doc-
trine became familiar."

(Hutchinson's " Hist. Mass. Bay," p. 264).

In " Franklin's Works" by Jared Sparks, vol. viii. p. 98, is a letter from Samuel Cooper to B. Franklin, dated Boston, 10th November, 1773, in which occurs the following:

"The speaker and many others in the House are your steady friends, particularly Major Hawley, from Northampton ; a gentleman of the law, who speaks with uncommon clearness and force, and is *behind no man there in point of influence.*"

[*f*] "1770. Several of the Council in the last election died [in note, "John Hill, Royal Tyler and Benjamin Lincoln, Esqrs."] or had resigned [in note, "Gamaliel Bradford and Joseph Hawley, Esqrs."], and their places were now filled with others who had the character of moderate men; the rest of the Council were the same persons who had been elected the last year." (Hutch. "Hist. Massachusetts Bay," p. 292).

[*g*] "1770. Mr. Otis, who for eight or nine years had greater influence than any other member, had been laid aside at the last election for the town, and Mr. Bowdoin had been chosen in his stead; but on Mr. Bowdoin being elected a councillor, Mr. John Adams succeeded him in the House. Mr. Hawley, member from Northampton, was equally, and perhaps more attended to; but Mr. Adams was more assiduous, and very politically proposed such measures only as he was well assured Mr. Hawley would join in." (*Ibidem*, pp. 292, 293).

The Document, "Broken Hints."

The following is taken verbatim from "Principles and Acts of the Revolution," H. Niles, Baltimore, 1822. (Copy in Mercantile Library Association, N. Y., 1849):

"Extracts of a letter from President Adams to H. Niles, dated Quincy, Feb. 5, 1819:

"DEAR SIR,—I enclose you the 'Broken Hints to be com-

municated to the Committee of Congress for the Massachusetts,'
by Major Joseph Hawley, of Northampton.

"This is the original paper that I read to Patrick Henry in
the fall of the year 1774, which produced his rapturous burst
of approbation and solemn asseveration, 'I am of that man's
mind.'

"I pray you to send it back to me. I would not exchange
this original for the show book of Harvard College, and printed
it shall be at my own expense in a hand bill."

"BROKEN HINTS TO BE COMMUNICATED TO THE COMMITTEE OF
CONGRESS FOR THE MASSACHUSETTS.

"We must fight, if we can't otherwise rid ourselves of British
taxation, all revenues and the constitution or form of government enacted for us by the British parliament. It is evil against
right, utterly intolerable to every man who has any idea or feel-
ing of right and liberty.

"It is easy to demonstrate that the Regulation Act will soon
annihilate every thing of value in the Charter, introduce perfect
despotism, and render the House of Representatives a mere form
and ministerial engine.

"It is now or never that we must assert our liberty. Twenty
years will make the number of Tories on this continent equal to
the number of Whigs. They who shall be born will not have an
idea of a free government.

"It will necessarily be a question, whether the new government of this province shall be suffered to take place at all, or
whether it shall be immediately withstood and resisted?

"A most important question this. I humbly conceive it not
best forcibly or wholly to resist it immediately. There is not
heat enough yet for the battle. Constant and a sort of negative
resistance of government, will increase the heat and blow the
fire. There is not military skill enough. That is improving,
and must be encouraged and improved, but will daily increase.

"Fight we must, finally, unless Britain retreats.

"But it is of infinite consequence that victory be the end and
the issue of hostilities. If we get to fighting before necessary dis-

positions are made for it, we shall be conquered and all will be lost forever.

"A certain clear plan for a constant, adequate and lasting supply of arms and military stores must be devised and fully contemplated. This is the main thing. This I think ought to be a capital branch of the business of Congress, to wit:—to devise and settle such a plan ; at least clearly to investigate how such supplies can be extensively had in case of need. While this is effecting, to wit:—while the continent is providing themselves with arms and military stores, and establishing a method for a sure and unfailing and constant supply, I conceive we had best to negotiate with Britain. If she will cede our rights and restore our liberties, all is well—every good man will rejoice ; if she will not agree to relinquish and abolish all American revenues, under every pretence and name, and all pretentions to order and regulate our internal policy and constitution ; then, if we have got any constant and sufficient supply of millitary stores, it will be time to take to arms. I can't quit this head—it ought to be immediately and most seriously attended to. It can't be any other than madness to commence hostilities before we have established resources on a sure plan for certain effectual military supplies. Men, in that case, will not be wanting.

"But what considerate man will ever consent to take up arms and go to war, where he has no reasonable assurance but that all must be given over and he fall a prey to the enemy, for want of military stores and ammunition, in a few weeks ?

"Either an effectual non-consumption agreement or resistance of the new government, will bring on hostilities very soon.

"1. As to a non-consumption agreement, it appears to me that it ought to be taken for certain truth that no plan of non-importation or consumption of tea, British goods in general, or enumerated articles, which is to rest or depend on the virtues of all the individuals, will succeed ; but must certainly prove abortive.

"The ministry will justly call such a plan futile, futile it will turn out; a plan of that sort may safely rest and be founded on the virtue of the majority, but then the majority, by the plan, must be directed to control the minority, which implies force. The plan therefore must direct and prescribe how that force shall be exercised.

"Those, again, who exercise that force, under the direction and by order of the majority, must by that majority be defended and indemnified.

"Dispositions must, therefore, necessarily be made to resist or overcome that force which will be brought against you—which will directly produce war and bloodshed.

"From thence it follows, that any non-consumption or non-importation plan which is not perfectly futile and ridiculous, implies hostilities and war.

"2. As to the resistance of the new government, that also implies war; for in order to resist and prevent the effect of the new government, it is indispensably necessary that the Charter government, or some other, must be maintained, constitutionally exercised and supported.

"The people will have some government or other. They will be drawn in by a seeming mild and just administration, which will last a while, legislation and executive justice must go on in some form or other, and we may depend on it they will; therefore the new goverment will take effect—until the old is restored.

"The old cannot be restored until the council take on them the administration, call assemblies, constitute courts, make sheriffs, etc. The council will not attempt this without good assurance of protection. This protection can't be given without hostilities. ·

"Our salvation depends upon an established, persevering union of the colonies.

"The tools of administration are using every device and effort to destroy that union, and they will certainly continue so to do. Thereupon, all possible desires and endeavours must be used to establish, improve, brighten and maintain such union.

"Every grievance of any one colony, must be held and considered by the whole as a grievance to the whole. This will be a difficult matter to effect, but it must be done.

"*Quere*, therefore, whether it is not absolutely necessary that some plan be settled for a continuation of congresses? But here we must be aware that congresses will soon be declared and enacted by parliament to be high treason.

"Is the India Company to be compensated or not? If to be compensated, each colony to pay the particular damage she has done, or is an average to be made on the Continent?

"The destruction of the tea was not unjust. Therefore, to what good purpose is the tea to be paid for, unless we are assured that, by so doing, our rights will be restored and peace obtained?

"What future measures is the Continent to preserve with regard to imported, dutied tea, whether it comes as East India property or otherwise, under the pretence and lie that the tea is imported from Holland, and the goods imported before a certain given day. Dutied tea will be imported and consumed—goods continue to be imported—your non-importation agreement eluded, rendered contemptible and ridiculous—unless all teas used, and all goods, are taken into some public custody, which will be inviolably faithful."

"[The foregoing is a literal copy of the venerable paper before me, except its frequent abbreviation of *the* and *that*, with the addition only of a few commas, etc., to make it read.—ED.]"

From the Boston Patriot.

Messrs. Ballard & Wright:

The enclosed letter from the venerable and patriotic Major Hawley (the author of the book, 'The Broken Hints'), has never been in print. Its publication at this time would perhaps not be irrelevant and would certainly gratify some of your country friends. It was written soon after the adoption of the present Constitution, and shows his opinion of that instrument. It is needless to add that we here think everything from the pen of that great man, deserving of record.   HAMPSHIRE.

To the Honourable the Senate of Massachusetts:

May it please your Honours: The intelligence given me by the writ of summons under the hand of the president of the council, that I am chosen a senator by a majority of the votes of the county of Hampshire, affords me a singular pleasure, on two accounts: The one is that an election to that high trust, by a majority of the unsolicited open suffrages of the voters of the county is a genuine proof of the good opinion of the people of my dear county; the other is that fair occasion it gives me to bear a free and public testimony against one part of our glorious constitution. I style it glorious, although I humbly conceive it has several great blemishes, on account whereof it will until corrected, be liable in my poor opinion, to very weighty exception; but still it remains glorious on account of the great quantity of excellent matter contained in it. That part of the constitution this event enables me not impertinently to except to, is the condition or term, which the constitution holds every one to, who has the honor to be elected a member of the general court of Massachusetts, before he may (as is expressed in the constitution) proceed to execute the duties of his place.

Be the person ever so immaculate and exemplary as a Christian; although he has, in the proper place, that is in the Christian Church, made a most solemn explicit and public profession of the Christian faith; though he has an hundred times, and continues perhaps every month in the year, by participating in the church of the body and blood of Christ, practically recognized and affirmed the sincerity of that profession; yet by the constitution, he is held, before he may be admitted to execute the duties of his office, to make and subscribe a profession of the Christian faith, or declaration that he is a Christian. Did our father-confessors imagine that a man, who has not so much fear of God in his heart as to restrain him from acting dishonestly and knavishly in the trust of a senator or representative, would hesitate a moment to subscribe that declaration? *Cui bono*, then, is the declaration? This extraordinary, not to say absurd, condition brings fresh to my mind a passage in the life of the pious, learned, and prudent Mr. John Howe, one of the strongest pillars of the dissenting interest in the reigns of Charles the 2d, and James the 2d. The history is as follows: that Mr. Howe, waiting upon a certain bishop, his lordship presently fell to expostulating with him about his nonconformity. Mr. Howe told him he could not have time without greatly trespassing on his patience to go through the objections he had to make to the terms of conformity. The bishop pressed him to name any one that he reckoned to be of weight. He instanced the point of re-ordination. "Why, pray, sir," said the bishop, "what hurt is there in being twice ordained?" "Hurt, my lord," says Mr. Howe to him, "the thought is shocking—it hurts my understanding. It is an absurdity, for nothing has two beginnings. I am sure," said he, "I am a minister of Christ, and I am ready to debate that matter with your lordship if you please; I cannot begin again to be a minister."

Besides, this term of executing the duties of the place is against common right, and as I may say, the natural franchise of every member of the commonwealth who has not by some crime or delictum forfeited his natural rights and franchises. It moreover reduces the ninth article of the declaration of rights to a mere futility, and in such a connection, it would be for the reputation of the declaration of rights if the same ninth article was wholly expunged. More than that, the said condition is plainly repugnant to the first great article of said declaration; and I am ready to debate that matter with any Doctor, who assisted in framing the constitution, either in convention or without doors. The said declaration of faith to be subscribed, which constitutes the said impolitic and unrighteous condition, will, I believe ever sound in every good ear almost as unearthly as the Session Justice's famous charge to the standing grand jury. Let us hear them successively:

"I do declare that I believe the Christian religion, and have a firm persuasion of its truth; and that I am seized and possessed in my own right of the property required by the constitution," &c.

"Gentlemen of the grand Jury: you are required by your oath to see to it, that the several towns in the county be provided, according to law, with

"Pounds and schoolmasters,
  Whipping posts and ministers."

Each containing an odd jumble of sacred and profane, but, to me, the charge jingles best by the constitution of the commonwealth of Massachusetts. I am, may it please your honors one of its senators; and I am strongly disposed, according to my poor abilities, to execute the duties of my office; but by the unconscionable not to 'say dishonorable terms, established by the same constitution, I am barred from endeavoring to perform these duties. I have been a professed Christian nearly forty years, and, although I have been guilty of many things unworthy of that character, whereof I am ashamed, yet I am not conscious that I have been guilty of anything wholly inconsistent with the truth of that profession.

The laws under the first charter required of the subjects of that state, in order to their enjoying some privileges, that they should be members in full communion of some Christian church. But it never was required in the Massachusetts Bay, that a subject, in order to his enjoying or exercising any franchise or office, should make profession of religion before a temporal court.

May it please your honours, we all heard of a lieut.-governor of the Massachusetts Bay, and some of us have known him very well, who contended long and earnestly that he had a right to a seat in council with a voice.

I imagine I can maintain a better argument than he did that I have a right to a seat in the senate of Massachusetts without a voice; but at present, I shall not attempt to take it.

I am, may it please your honours, with the greatest respect to the senate, your most obedient humble servant,

October 28, 1780.   JOSEPH HAWLEY.

The following letters are copied from Peter Force's "American Archives" :

Letters of Major Hawley to Elbridge Gerry.

WATERTOWN, February 18, 1776.*

DEAR SIR : I hope you will forgive me if I herein appear indelicate, by attempting to inculcate some things which I hinted

*Fourth Series, iv. 1190.

to you in the minutes which you was pleased to accept of me, as you was setting out on your journey to Congress. But if you knew the infinite weight they are on my mind, you would not blame me, whether they impressed your mind in like manner or not. One was that the most seasonable and effectual care should be taken that a sufficient number of the best of troops should be seasonably marched into Canada, and thorough provision made for their subsistence, pay and clothing, full supplies of artillery, arms and ammunition, that they be sure to repel and overcome all the efforts of the enemy in that quarter the approaching season. Depend on it, that the efforts of the enemy there and at New York the next season will be the greatest and the earliest which they can possibly make. In the year 1760, I am certain that ships arrived at Quebeck from England some time in April, and I think as early as the middle of April, if not earlier. If they have any judgment or policy in England, their land forces for the reduction of America will be chiefly employed by the way of Quebeck and New York; diversions may be given in other ports, but their main strength will be destined hither. I have no doubt but you are, by this time, fully sensible that the sharpest eye must be unremittedly kept on the people of New York; their manœuvres and tergiversations exceed the depths of Satan. But I will not school you any longer on this head.

I beg leave to let you know that I have read the pamphlet, entitled "Common Sense," addressed to the inhabitants of America, and that every sentiment has sunk into my well-prepared heart; in short, you know that my heart before was like good ground well prepared for good seed; and without an American Independent Supreme Government and Constitution, wisely devised and designed, well established and settled, we shall always be but a rope of sand; but that well done, invincible. I must not repeat what I said to you of the worthlessnes and futility of all paper currency, without such a general, well established and independent government.

Your field of business is immense, and absolutely boundless; but industry, courage, application and perseverance, will surmount everything; some relaxation and exercise is absolutely necessary to maintain health and spirit; but sloth and dissipation, and turning off business to others, and procrastination, if they gain any admission, will be our infallible ruin. I know you will not indulge to them, and I hope none others of your number. Solomon never uttered a truer maxim than when he said "Confidence in an unfaithful man, in time of trouble, is like a broken tooth, and a foot out of joint."

Two things I beg leave to hint; the one is, that it seemed to us here that when Congress, by their late resolve, ordered an appeal from our Admiralty Courts to their honorable body, they did not well consider how dissonant such a mode of trial is from the genius of the times, to wit, by Jury; nor how much it is open to the exception which was made to the Stamp Act, of its exposing and making one of the parties liable to be carried for a trial to any remote quarter or part of the Continent, at the will of a Crown officer. Would it not have been more expedient and constitutional to have ordered the appeal to have been to the Superior Court of the Colony in which the first trial was had ? Besides, it seems to bear hard on the maxim, " That the Legislature and Executive ought always to be distinct and diverse."

Secondly, I hope, Sir, you will by no means forget to endeavor that there be the most peremptory and absolute order and injunction on all the generals and officers of the American Army, that quarters for the army, or any part of them, shall in no case be impressed, but by the intervention of civil magistrate, or direction of the Legislature of the Colony. They have again (I suppose through the resentment of Park, the Assistant Quartermaster) quartered a company on Major Thompson, against his will. Our Assembly is so much on the wing, and the active members so generally gone, that it is impossible to make any proper remonstrance thereof to the General.

It is not easy to imagine what a handle such conduct as this gives to the Tories, and how much they rejoice to be able to take such exceptions; besides it is downright and intolerably wrong. It is much more necessary that Congress should make

43

some express order and regulation for their forces in every part, touching their behaviour in this particular, because you know that the Colonies in general and this in particular, are in the hands and power of the army, by reason of the militia being, in a great degree, stripped of their arms and ammunition, for the sake of furnishing the army.

I suggest one thing more, and I have done, to wit: I hope that the next period or term for which the Continental troops will be inlisted, will be three, or at least two years; the disadvantages and risk of their being engaged and held for so short terms, even for but one whole year, are many; at the same time they never will, nor can I say that I desire that they should engage for an indefinite time; but I believe they will after a little while, be willing to engage for two or three years.

My letter is unconnected. I enter matters as they occur, without studying coherence; If you think them of any value, you have full leave to communicate to your brethren of this Colony.

I am, Sir, with great and most sincere respect,

Your obedient humble servant,

To Mr. Gerry.   JOSEPH HAWLEY.

February 20, 1776.*

Pray Sir, will it not be extremely difficult for us to hold on with our defense, and support all our inhabitants without trade? Will people who have been bred and accustomed to trade till they have arrived at men's and women's estate, ever get into any other business? Be sure they never will be dexterous at any other, nor contented; nay, they will be a weight on the community, and a very heavy one too. But if we resolve on independence, what will hinder but that we may instantly commence a trade, not only with Holland, France and Spain, but with all the world, as the government of the new independent state shall permit. Then we shall have done with the unmanageable plans and chimeras of non-importation agreements, which, with non-consumption agreements, never were and never will be kept, and tend inexpressibly to debauch and wickedize a people, by means of the irresistable temptation which trading people will always be under to violate the general agreements, not only for the sake of profits, but really for any reputable subsistence; whereas, the instant you resolve on independence, and give leave to trade, your trading people will immediately fly to it, whatever risks and hazards there may be of losing; and indeed, the greatest part will escape.

Pray consider this matter, with regard to Canada and the Dutch of New York. Will they ever join with us heartily, who, in order to do it, must sacrifice their trade, to which they are so much addicted, and whereby they have always made good profits, and expose themselves to want and beggary? Whereas, the moment that we resolve on independence, trade will be free for them—for the one to France and the other to Holland; to which they always inclined, and would heretofore go at almost as great risks as they will then at first run; then we shall have done with our impracticable associations for non-consumption, the source of infinite feuds and animosity.

Independence, in short, is the only way to union and harmony, to vigor and despatch in business; our eye would be single, and our whole body full of light; anything short of it will, as appears to me, be our destruction, infalable destruction, and that speedily. Amen.

To Mr. Gerry. JOSEPH HAWLEY.

WATERTOWN, May 1, 1776.*

MY DEAR SIR : The Tories dread a declaration of independence, and a course of conduct on that plan, more than death. They console themselves with a belief that the Southern colonies will not accede to it. My hand and heart are full of it. There will be no abiding union without it. When the colonies come to be pressed with taxes, they will divide and crumble to pieces. Will a government stand on recommendations? It is idle to

suppose so. Will Canada ever join us without Independence
and Government? They will not. Can we subsist, and support
our trading people, without trade? It appears more and more
every day, in the country and Army, that we cannot. Nay,
without a real Continental Government our Army will overrun
us, and people will, by and by, sooner than you may be aware of,
call for their old Constitutions; and as they did in England after
Cromwell's death, call in Charles the Second. For God's sake
let there be a full Revolution, or all has been done in vain. Independence and a well planned Continental Government, will
save us. God bless you. Amen and Amen.

To Elbridge Gerry. JOSEPH HAWLEY.

WATERTOWN, June 13, 1776.*

DEAR SIR: Last week I received your valued and much
esteemed favor of 25th May, and marked all the contents; and
notwithstanding delays and impediments which you mention, I
yet flatter myself that your Congress, like the Calvinistick Christian, will go on from one degree of grace to another, till you ar-
rive at perfection. You know that a great part of the pleasures
of life arises from surmounting difficulties and overcoming
opposition.

You cannot declare Independence too soon; but the Confederation must be formed with great deliberation. When the
House here called, last week, for the instructions of the several
towns touching Independency, agreeable to the recommendation
of the last House (which recommendation you undoubtedly saw
in the Watertown newspapers), it appeared that about two-thirds
of the towns in the Colony had met, and all instructed in the
affirmative and generally returned to be unanimously. As to
the other towns, the accounts of their members were, either that
they were about to meet, or that they had not received the notice,
as it was given only in the newspapers. Whereupon the House
immediately ordered the unnotified towns to be notified by hand
bills, and in a short time undoubtedly we shall have returns

from all; and it is almost certain that the returns will be universally to support Congress, with their lives and fortunes, in case of declaration of Independence.

Yesterday our Assembly resolved the requisition of five thousand men for New York and Canada. The House immediately appointed a committee to devise the manner of raising them, and with the utmost assiduity the Court will pursue it till accomplished.

I am your most assured friend and servant,

To Elbridge Gerry, Esquire.   JOSEPH HAWLEY.

Letters of Major Hawley to General Gates.

NORTHAMPTON, August 14, 1776.*

GENERAL GATES: I this minute received your favour of the 10th instant, and carefully mark the contents, and shall, dear sir, do everything in my power as soon as possible to effect what you have been pleased to ask. Your Honor will please to be informed that Number Four is upwards of seventy miles from this place. It is directly counter to the orders of the Council of this Government, that a man should tarry to inoculate. I have been so happy as to effect the march of about seven hundred good men from this county, without any delay for inoculation.

I have the honour to be, with the greatest respect, your most obedient, humble servant,

JOSEPH HAWLEY.

NORTHAMPTON, August 20, 1776.†

MAY IT PLEASE YOUR HONOUR: As it is proper that you should be made acquainted with the terms upon which all the men under your command have engaged in the service, and as it may have happened that our Council, through the multiplicity of business, may have neglected to transmit to you the resolve of the General Assembly upon which our first recruits for our

Army were raised, your Honour will not consider me as officious in sending to you that resolve.

You will observe, Sir, that the non-commissioned officers, as well as the privates, are entitled to a month's advance pay ; and I beg leave to inform you that as, in some companies which went from the County of Hampshire, the non-commissioned officers were not appointed when they marched, they have not received any more advance pay than that of private soldiers. That was the case in Capt. Lyman's company, and I take it to have been so in Capt. Gray's. Pursuant to an after-resolve (of which I am not possessed), the commission officers were to have a month's advance pay, which those from this county have generally received.

I have many things on my mind which I want to suggest, but will defer them to another opportunity.

I most heartily wish your Honour health, victory, and on every account, a happy campaign ; and have the honour to be, with the greatest respect, your most obedient and humble servant,

To General Gates.   JOSEPH HAWLEY.

P. S.—According to your desire, Sir, I have done everything in my power to suppress the pernicious and iniquitous practice of delaying the march of officers and soldiers for the sake of taking the small-pox.   Yours,   J. H.

NORTHAMPTON, October 6, 1776.

MAY IT PLEASE YOUR HONOUR : I am so well knowing to your humanity and the goodness of your natural temper, as to be assured that nothing within your power necessary to the safety and health of the troops under our command will be omitted. I only beg leave just to acquaint you that from the declarations of officers in your army and people who visit your camps, the country are made vastly uneasy at being informed that there is scarcely any medicines for the sick, and that it is rare that any rations are dealt out to the privates but of meat and bread, or any money paid in lieu of the other articles. They say that there are plenty of doctors, but no medicine. Your Honour knows whether there are any grounds for these complaints, and if there are, whether these defects are chargeable on the Congress, or the neglects, frauds, and dishonesty of such as are employed by them.

I have heretofore suggested to your Honour the speedy need your army will be of snow-shoes; and as every little helps in every case, I mentioned in one or two former letters that I had by accident, in my custody, between fifty and sixty pair of snow-shoes, in good condition, belonging to the States, purchased last winter by Mr. Mifflin.

I have the honour to be, with the greatest respect, your Honour's most obedient, humble servant,

To General Gates.   JOSEPH HAWLEY.

Elbridge Gerry to General Warren.

PHILADELPHIA, July 5, 1776.*

DEAR SIR: I have the pleasure to inform you that a determined resolution of the Delegates from some of the Colonies to push the question of independency, has had a most happy effect, and, after a day's debate, all the Colonies excepting New York, whose Delegates are not empowered to give either an affirmative or negative voice, united in declaration long sought for, solicited, and necessary—the Declaration of Independence.

New York will most probably, on Monday next, when its convention meets for forming a Constitution, join in the measure, and then it will be entitled THE UNANIMOUS DECLARATION OF THE THIRTEEN STATES OF AMERICA.

I enclose you a copy of the Declaration for yourself, and another for Major Hawley, and offer you my sincere congratulations on the occasion; and I pray that we may never want the Divine aid, or the spirit and means to defend it.

Yours, &c.,   ELBRIDGE GERRY.

[A letter of John Adams to Major Hawley (never before published), and a letter from Major Hawley to Rev. Mr. Hall of Sutton, with other interesting historical matter, are omitted from this Sketch for want of room, but appear in full in the " HAWLEY RECORD."]

www.ingramcontent.com/pod-product-compliance
Lightning Source LLC
Chambersburg PA
CBHW030906260626
47169CB00008B/2706